The Spanking Sin:

A Story of Desire and Redemption

Vivian MacKenzie

DEDICATION

To my amazing husband, without whom this book would never exist. And to any reader who finds themselves in these pages.

INTRODUCTION

Imagine being alone on a desert island and finding a beautiful bottle. Upon inspection, the bottle opens to reveal a misty Genie bowing and promising three wishes with all the usual caveats. What would those wishes be? Money? Power? Sex? World peace? Alice knew what she would choose. It would be to rid herself of the one thing that had plagued her for her whole life: The Spanking Sin.

Alice didn't know why she had something wrong with her. She grew up in a normal family in a normal town with a normal, rainbow bedspread on her bed and a normal non-descript, mop-like mutt running around the cyclone fenced yard. Even her name was plain and practical— Alice Maude Brown. Her middle name was perhaps the most interesting part of her name, and it came from one of her more interesting of grandmothers. Alice had married young and raised a family; Maude was rumored to have been a dancing girl at one point. Alice grew up being good at math, playing catcher on a softball team, and eating entirely too much pizza for her own good. She went to the prescribed state college for the prescribed time and attended the prescribed drinking parties. Apart from a college religious experience that entrenched her firmly in the camp of bible-believing evangelicals, her life looked boring and predictable for the most part.

Aside from one thing, of course. Her secret shame, her thorn in her side, her Something Wrong. The one thing she would change if the Genie asked her, or if God would answer her numerous prayers on the subject, as she termed it, in her own head, as the "Spanking Sin." She did not know how that sin had come about. Growing up with a voracious appetite for books and reading almost everything that stocked the little library at her school, she read from morning to night. She remembered being in first grade and reading the *Little House on the Prairie* books and being mesmerized by the incidents of punishments in them. To the current day the words, "And he whipped Laura with the strap" were emblazoned on her psyche. She looked up "spank" in the dictionary and got a little thrill on seeing the word in print. And though it shamed her, and she would never admit it, she was always on the lookout for stories with spanking in it. She could, to that day, list of childhood books with a spanking in it— everything from *Oliver Twist* to *A Charmed Life*. Movies and television as well—*Little House on the Prairie, Bonanza, Pete's Dragon*. But it was never enough, and never exactly how she wanted it to go. So instead, she began writing.

The stories she wrote were private, and she never showed anybody. When her mom or friends became too suspicious, she would write a story with no spanking in it to share with them, and some of those stories she ended up liking very much as well. But always she felt compelled and drawn toward the ones with spanking in them. By the time she went to college she had over thirty notebooks filled with those stories, and quickly moved to writing them on the laptop she got for high school graduation. The freedom of having her own laptop all to herself for the first time was intoxicating—that wasn't one she had to share with a sibling or turn back into school; it was hers. But in a moment of shame and repentance, she burned those notebook stories and deleted them from her hard drive some time during Junior year. She then abstained from writing for nearly a year, but then with shame, she gave in and began writing again.

And just to be clear— she didn't recognize that there was anything sexual about these fantasies. She would have fantasies about sex, but those were different, more compelling and more intense. But she craved a spanking in a different and deeper way—and her own attempts at smacking her own bottom were quite unsatisfactory. And so, she lived vicariously through her characters, jealous for what they had, and she did not, though they were not generally appreciative of their punishments. Her stories and strict and loving fathers, evil and abusive fathers that children needed to be rescued from, teens and young adults trying to figure out their lives, and the bravery of presenting their backside for punishment.

In college, she studied Psychology—as everyone else who wonders what the hell is wrong with them does. She went into a clinical and ultimately unemotional graduate program, and soon she was termed an expert in mental health—though she could never figure out her own. In her own therapy, she could never reveal her predilection, and so never got help figuring out what was wrong with her. She had hinted at it with a mentor in her church as an undergraduate, but even that little bit sent her scurrying back to her hole. Though the mentor was kind and gracious, she didn't understand. She did papers in school on BDSM and sexual deviancies, but not feeling that what she craved matched up with the leather and dungeons that seemed to represent people who had a similar predilection to her.

And then she met Barney at church the summer she turned twenty-four. He was handsome-ish, kind-hearted, and fun. She found herself sailing the lake with him, eating sushi with him, and soon was head-over-heels in love with him. She told herself that maybe marrying and having a satisfying sex life would finally rid her of those bothersome fantasies, and that she would be able to leave that embarrassing part of her life behind. And so, she married this kind man, promising herself to push down The Spanking Sin until it couldn't possibly infringe on her happy life. She would live the life of a Seattle newlywed—setting up their little apartment perfectly, hosting dinners and parties for friends, and in general being the woman her husband thought he'd married. She knew at some instinctual level that her strait-laced, religiously devout husband would never understand her Spanking Sin, and she couldn't bear the thought of him thinking less of her. So, she went to her marriage bed a virgin; bent on hiding what she thought was wrong with her and let the unbridled joy of discovering sex with her equally virginal husband take over her joy.

And it was a joy; so much more so than she had imagined. So, there she was in a job that suited her, a happy and satisfying marriage, prospects of buying a house, and having kids, and a circle of friends. And nobody knew that she secretly replayed the scene in *Community* where one of the main characters gets spanked with a switch by another character's grandmother. She never read *Fifty Shades of Grey* because it felt un-Christian, she was careful to stay off websites that might be interpreted as porn, and she secretly reveled in reading a certain type of fanfiction.

But that was all until she found, at the ripe old age of twenty-nine, the Emerald City Therapeutic Massage.

CHAPTER ONE

Emerald City Therapeutic Massage was in a non-descript, clinical building just north of downtown Seattle. There was a waiting room, a receptionist, and fluorescent lights. A run-in with a particularly difficult schizophrenic patient made Alice's supervisor ask her about self-care, and after a mild scolding from her boss, Alice booked an appointment. In school, they had continually taught that self-care was the key to surviving the job as a therapist, otherwise working with people and their problems would lead to burn out.

"You aren't seeing a therapist anymore, are you?" Bridgett had asked Alice with her clear-eyed intuition. "You don't leave early on Thursdays anymore."

"I just felt as if we were in a stopping place," Alice told her, of course not adding that the stopping place had arisen due to her inability to tell her therapist what was really bothering her. She had grown weary of dodging her questions and keeping herself hidden.

"Do you have time to do any of your hobbies?" she asked. "You know how important self-care is."

"Yes, I know," she replied with a smile and a shrug. "I do a few things." *Did writing fanfiction where Snape spanks Harry count as a hobby? Because if so, I just got fourteen reviews on my latest chapter.*

"You know, I like a good massage," Bridgett mused. "I find it helps a lot. Should I give you the number of where I go?"

"There's a place by me I've been wanting to try," Alice said trying to remember the name. Something about Emerald City?

"Good, I'm glad to hear that," she said in a business-like fashion issuing a command more than acknowledging a wish. "I'll ask you next week how it went."

With chagrin, Alice realized then that she would have to actually do it. Bridgett was kind and reasonable as a supervisor, but she was also persistent. She knew that she would either have to go back to therapy or try massage, but her boss wasn't going to take her doing nothing as adequate professional self-care. And so, Alice found herself walking into the massage clinic a few days later, not knowing why she felt so embarrassed doing so. Wasn't massage a normal thing people did?

"Hello," the cheerful, middle-aged woman at the front desk greeted her.

"Hi," she smiled back. "I'm here for a massage."

"Therapeutic spanking or massage?" she asked without a blink.

"What?" she asked her cheeks blazing. "I'm not sure I heard you right."

"We offer therapeutic spanking as well as massage," she told me unruffled.

"Massage," she barely breathed, her breath choking. "I'm here for a therapeutic massage."

"Would you like me to give you a pamphlet about our spanking services as well?" she asked as if she were asking what her insurance coverage was.

"Er, sure," she told her, deadly curious but not trying to show she was.

"Fill out this paperwork," she told Alice. "If you decide you want the spanking services there's another form as well."

"Oh, okay," Alice answered knowing that her face was blazing red. How could the woman talk so casually about it?

Alice sat and filled out the form, her eyes drifting to the spanking pamphlet. Shoving the pamphlet into her purse, she focused on the paperwork and on the massage she was going to get. In truth, she had never had a massage apart from the backrubs people casually give to each other in college, so she had enough trepidation to begin with.

"Your therapist today will be Mike," the receptionist chirped at Alice when she returned the form.

"Can't I have a woman?" she asked, shocked. It never occurred to her that she would have a male massage therapist.

"We don't have any women free today," the receptionist merrily replied. "We could reschedule for tomorrow if you want a woman. But don't worry honey, it's very professional here. Mike has a fatherly way about it him; you won't mind a bit."

"Fatherly?" she choked a bit. On top of all the talk about spanking, "fatherly" seemed the last thing she wanted to describe her massage therapist as.

"Are you all right?" she asked looking Alice up and down with concern. "Do you need some water?"

"Water would be great," Alice replied regaining her voice. She told herself that this was professional, and she understood that the difference between a male therapist and a female shouldn't matter. Alice had clients all the time wanted a woman or a man for their psychotherapist, and her profession wasn't touching their mostly naked bodies.

Sipping the water the receptionist helpfully supplied, she calmed. *This will be fine,* she firmly told herself. *I am a grown-up and a professional.*

"Come on back, then," the receptionist directed. "Go ahead and change into a robe."

"Do I have to take off my clothes?" she asked suddenly embarrassed again.

"You can leave your panties on if you're shy," she told her with a wink. "However, you're comfortable; but it's easier the fewer clothes wear."

"Okay," Alice agreed cursing Bridgett as she entered the dressing room. She should have warned her about that part.

As she changed, she heard the receptionist greet another woman who came into the changing area. "Hi, Trish," she greeted. "Looks like you got a good one today."

"I'll be lucky to sit for dinner," the woman answered wryly. "But yes, it was just right. Mike knows what he's doing."

Alice's heart started thumping. Was that the same man that would do her massage? Had this woman just been actually spanked? All too easily she pictured the voice she heard as a sexy blond upended over the lap of a large, muscular Italian man. *Wait, make it a fatherly, muscular Italian man.*

"I like Tony myself," the receptionist answered. "But I like it softer, and I like a lower back massage afterwards, and he's good at those."

"Mike has large, hard hands," Trish laughed. "So good. You almost don't need a paddle with him. And he's great at hitting that sweet spot."

"Next week same time?" she asked. "Or is that the week you're on vacation?"

"Vacation is the week after next," Trish replied. "Normal time next week."

"Great, I'll get that on the books then."

Alice exited the waiting room trying to look hip and urban and not as if the woman she was about to meet had actually just been spanked. Her eyes grew wide upon seeing a woman in full medieval dress. She was not the sexy blond in high heels that Alice had pictured, but rather a very normal-looking woman a few years older than her with soft, brown hair.

Laughing softly at Alice's surprise, the woman smoothed her dress. "Pretty, isn't it? This is one of my favorite scenarios."

"Scenarios?" Alice asked still in shock.

"Yes," she answered. "Next week, I think I'm doing the cowgirl one again. That's one of my favorites, too. This place has great scenarios, and you can do your own as well."

"That sounds great," Alice replied trying to sound at ease but secretly wondering if a person could die of shame. How could that possibly be therapeutic for her? Although, she had to admit that there was also something burning in her stomach as well, something that felt intensely attractive.

"I'll show you to your room," the receptionist cheerfully directed. "Mike will be with you shortly."

"Okay," she agreed weakly as the receptionist showed her into a lavender-scented room with low lights and Zen music playing.

"You can lie on the table and relax," she told her. "Let the lavender calm you. It's good to have a few minutes to find your center before a massage."

"Thanks," Alice answered, and with a smile, the woman exited the room. She felt a surge of warmth for the practical receptionist, and also an urge to find her purse and read the pamphlet she had given her. Alice had so many questions. But she didn't want Mike to come in to find her reading the pamphlet, so she forced herself to lay on the table, stomach-down, and listen to the soft music.

"Hello," a deep male voice greeted her. "My name is Mike, and I will be your therapist today."

"Hi Mike," she greeted him coming half off the table and turning her head to sneak a sideways look at a very ordinary looking middle-aged man. "I've never, well, I've never done this before."

"That's okay," he told her. "There's a first time for everything. Just lay down and let me work my magic."

"Magic?" she squeaked.

"You are a jumpy little thing," he laughed at her. "Lay back down, my dear."

There was a note of command in his voice that made

her stomach jump. It wasn't necessarily stern, just a note of strength. She found herself responding to his voice and felt her stomach melt.

"I saw your last customer in the dressing room," Alice blurted as she tried to relax hoping that he wouldn't see her blush.

"I can't talk about other customers, of course," he replied easily beginning to massage her neck. "But let's just say I sure enjoy my work."

"I've never heard of a place that does spanking," she said softly.

"It's a unique niche that's for sure," Mike replied. "But it's just another form of release for people, not too different than what we do for massage really, just a form of deep tissue massage. With a fantasy element, of course."

"Is that mainly what you do here?"

"No, we do a lot of normal massages like what we're doing now," Mike said working his way down her spine. "But we started offering spanking services a few years ago and the business has grown quite a bit. Turns out there are a lot of people that just really want to be spanked and not have to worry about safety, meeting strangers, or people expecting sex. We are a strictly non-sexual, therapeutic spanking service. Nobody's naked unless the customer chooses a bare bottom, there's no touching or fondling. You can just have a straight spanking or have one in the context of a story, it's your choice."

"I've never heard of this," Alice confessed wishing she had.

"Well, it's a fantasy for a lot of people," Mike explained working the muscles of her shoulder. "A lot of people that work high-powered jobs just like to have something physical where they don't feel in control. A lot of people have guilt which it helps alleviate, and a lot of people have just always wanted the experience and really couldn't tell you why."

"Is it expensive?" she asked with some trepidation.

"We charge a bit extra for costumes," he admitted. "But really it's nearly the same price as a massage."

"It sounds interesting," she said noncommittally. Was she really ready to just admit to a stranger a longing she had yet to admit to her husband?

"If you're interested, I have an informational packet that has more than the pamphlet," he told her. "I'll make sure you get one on the way out. It sounds like I might have you over my knee soon."

"Aren't I, you know, big for that?" Alice asked blushing as she thought of her size 16 butt. But the way he delivered that comment made her entire insides feel alive.

"Of course not," he laughed. "I've had a 450-pound man over my lap. Size doesn't matter."

"Oh," she answered feeling stupid. Alice then concentrated on the soft music as Mike massaged her muscles, lifting the towel that covered her bottom. In a very business-like manner, he massaged her thighs and legs, and she found herself relaxing into the touch. But her mind was a whirl of questions and desires that she could barely even admit to herself.

"The massage is nearly done," Mike told Alice waking her from her stupor of fantasies. "I could never, of course, give you a real spanking without the proper consents signed, but since you seem interested would you like me to give you a few light swats to see if it's something you would like? Sometimes the fantasy differs greatly from the reality, so it might be good to know before you book an appointment."

She hesitated, and then answered without looking at him, "Sure! That sounds great." She was struck by how false her voice sounded, as if someone had just offered her a dinner of liver and green beans and she was trying to be polite. But she also knew how desperately she wanted that, and her stomach clenched in anticipation.

Alice felt him lift the towel, uncover her bottom, and she clenched her eyes hard. Her heart pounded so hard she thought it might be audible.

"Relax, little one," he told her softly, gently placing his hand on her lower back, just above her panty-clad bottom. "Just two gentle swats. I'll check with you after the first one to make sure you want the second."

Alice nodded feeling unable to breathe, but she found her bottom relaxing under his gentle hand.

"Here it is," he told her, and she felt his large hand swat her on one of her cheeks, just hard enough to tingle. "Do you want the other swat, too?"

"Yes," she choked out, barely believing that was happening to her.

He answered with another swat, slightly firmer, on the other cheek. She let out a small gasp at the resulting tingle.

"You liked that," she heard his gentle voice assure her. "Didn't you?"

"Yes," she replied, startled into honesty. How she wished that she could say that she didn't.

"It's nothing to be ashamed of," he told her gently. "I see many people that are ashamed, but I see it as just the way some people are built. It's like some people liking spicy food, or some people being afraid of swimming. it's just how you are."

"Thanks," she replied, not believing him but wishing that she could.

"I have a few regular openings in my schedule," he told her casually. "Just call in and make an appointment if you're interested."

Interested? The man had no idea.

CHAPTER TWO

That night Alice lay back, satisfied and tousled, thinking about what had transpired that afternoon and wishing she could just tell her husband about it.

"Well, someone was certainly in the mood," he laughed lying beside her and drawing her in for a cuddle. "I think that massage you had today really relaxed you."

"Bridgett said that I might think about regular massage for self-care," she told him feeling like she was lying. "That's what she does. I thought maybe I'd give it a try instead of counselling for a while."

"Sounds nice," he said nuzzling her neck. "Does our insurance cover it?"

"Unfortunately, no," she answered sounding casual. "But it's not too expensive, maybe we could try twice a month to start?"

"Sure," he answered. "Sounds like something you have to do. And if I get enthusiastic sex like this out of it, I'm happy."

"It was rather nice," Alice answered feeling a little smug. Her thighs were still twitching from the aftereffects of her second orgasm. And she couldn't help but think of that tingle Mike had applied to her bottom earlier that day, and her stomach squirmed.

"Hmm, now I'm all sleepy," he mumbled nipping her ear and absently fingering her nipple. "Do you have an alarm set for tomorrow?"

"I do," she answered feeling sleepy herself. Though the sex with her husband had been satisfying just as it always was, she couldn't help but wish she could have more with him. Alice was used to keeping the Spanking Sin away from Barney, but she started to feel a twinge of regret that she had to do it. *Mike now knows something about me that my own husband doesn't.* and that rankled. When it was a secret from everyone, it felt different, like she could deny she had it. But now . . .

"If you could choose to try any new thing sexually, what would you do?" she asked him finding herself hoping again that giving her a spanking was in his fantasies.

"I like it when you wear that little G-string," he admitted. "Especially with that see-thru skirt you have. Just at home, of course."

"Of course," she answered, secretly disappointed.

"Hmm," he snuggled in.

"Don't you ever wish for something else?" she asked. "Like some secret sexual fantasy you always wished for?"

"I think my sexual fantasy growing up was always just to actually have sex," he laughed. "You know, with a real live girl. I don't know. Are you trying to ask about oral sex again?"

"Maybe," she answered, trying not to raise his suspicions.

"Well, our anniversary is coming up," he reasoned. "Maybe we could go stay at that place on Camano Island again. You know, the one with the big bathtub? Maybe some experimentation would be a good idea."

"I think that sounds good," she smiled inwardly.

"Some people think that it's not Godly," he answered. "But really, as long as you're not feeling somehow degraded by it, it should be fine, right? But if you don't like it, just tell me."

"Okay," she agreed.

"I saw a movie once," he mused stroking her shoulder gently. "The main character was a mobster, and he was seeing a therapist. Anyway, she asked him why he had a mistress, and he said because he didn't want his wife's mouth to be doing that and also kissing his kids."

"Do you think that?" she asked, curious.

"No, not really," he answered. "But I just want to make sure, you know, that you're okay with it. I would hate for you to feel you had to, you know, please me if you didn't like it. And I want to be, you know, clean and everything. That's why I was thinking about the bathtub at that little inn."

"I'll let you know," she promised. "And besides, we have no kids to kiss."

"Well, many more rolls in the hay like that one," he laughed, "and I would say we had come by one honestly, even on birth control."

"Ha ha," she agreed with a bemused smile.

Alice didn't know how she would have answered if he had asked her if she had any fantasies. She felt herself tensing in readiness for the question. Would she have answered him? But instead, his body slipped away from hers, just a little at a time, and soon she heard him softly snoring. Pulling the blanket around herself, she wished that she could drift off as easily as he could. Instead, she crept from the bed pulling on her soft cotton nightie and found the booklet Mike gave her tucked discreetly under the sanitary supplies in the bathroom drawer. She had actually put the pamphlet inside the box of pads and then covered it, assuming that would be the best place to hide it from accidental discovery. The pamphlet itself was plain and non-descript showing the hands of a therapist on an unidentifiable part of someone's body as if they were offering spa services.

Alice opened the booklet and surprised by how professional it all looked. The policies looked simple as well, and made her feel better. They believed spanking could be part of a healing process or just a release of stress or anxiety. Though they recognized that spanking could often be erotic and linked to sex, they emphasized that the spanking services they offered were therapeutic in nature and not sexual. The booklet went on to say, "Many people seek our services as a way to work out internal issues. Often people don't know why they are attracted to the idea of spanking. Sometimes people are not able to express those longings to their intimate partners and trying to find someone who might be able to spank them looks like navigating very frightening worlds of trusting complete strangers. Our clinic is designed to meet this spiritual need, to reduce stress and anxiety in the client, and to offer this therapy in a safe, clinical setting."

Alice's heart skipped a beat. This booklet knew who she was! There were others like her! She crept with the booklet back to her bed, careful not to wake up her husband. She continued to read in surreptitious excitement. "We also recognize a necessary element of play and fun in spanking," the booklet went on the explain. "Clients can always choose the straight spanking with no fantasy elements, but we also offer scenarios that can either be performed as written or can be tailored to the specific client. Including fantasy in spanking can make the experience more meaningful and personal to the client. Have you ever wanted to be spanked as a naughty medieval prince or princess, or a rough and rowdy cowgirl or boy? How about a misbehaving maid or the classic school student? Or would you like a tantric spanking complete with mantras, candles and a massage afterwards? Bring your fantasies to us and let us help make them come to life."

Alice blinked. Picturing herself in a plaid skirt—a real one, not the "sexy" ones in costume shops—and bending over Mike's lap made her stomach squirm so much that she thought that she was going to faint. White cotton underwear, exposed as he flipped up her skirt, as his hand reddened her bottom . . .

"It's late," she heard Barney mumble from the other side of the bed. "Aren't you going to sleep?"

"Of course," she answered clicking off her light and slipping the booklet inside another book beside the bed. "Goodnight, honey."

"Night," he mumbled and soon was snoring again. It felt like hours to Alice before she was able to join him.

The next day Alice found herself waiting with great anticipation until nine A.M. to call the clinic. But she didn't want to call right at nine. Wouldn't that signal that she was too eager? Would nine fifteen show enough casual indifference that she was not like some crazy, sex-starved teenager?

Alice decided to settle for nine twenty-two, and got right through to the perky receptionist from the day before. "We have an opening next week with Mike on Thursday at five P.M." she told her. "Would this be for the therapeutic spanking or for massage?"

"Um, spanking," Alice answered said glancing around her empty office as if someone might overhear.

"I'll send you the menu, then," the receptionist told her. "It's a secure link to a page that asks you what you want. Just fill out your preferences, so we can set up for you. For newbies the therapist usually likes having a conversation beforehand, just to manage expectations and everything. That means we don't book sessions for less than an hour for first timers."

"Okay," she answered hesitantly.

"Make sure you fill it out by Friday," she chirped. "And if you have any questions, don't hesitate to call. For first-timers, we recommend either using a gentle implement or the hand, and we also recommend nothing over the intensity level of five."

"Okay, thanks," she said as if she were booking an appointment to get her hair done.

Alice waited with trepidation for the email to come wondering what a "menu" could possibly be. When it came and she clicked on it, she found even more reason to blush. It had details of the different scenarios and what they would entail, as well as questions such as positions, implements, and pain levels. It all looked so overwhelming, so Alice decided to go with the first stirring of fantasy that she received when she read it and clicked on the schoolgirl scenario.

"The schoolgirl scenario is one of our most popular," the menu read. "It is classically set up as the 18-year-old senior in high school is brought into the principal's office for one of the various offences, which you may choose."

Alice found herself choosing caught skipping school, to be spanked over his knee on the couch with his hand, and to have her skirt up but her panties to remain on. She blushed at the idea of baring her bottom but decided that she would start conservatively. With chagrin, Alice already realized that she would go again. She also signed up for massage aftercare, assuming it would feel comforting to have it. Then there was the question of escalating consequences—would she allow him to increase the intensity level, use an implement, or bare her bottom if she didn't cooperate? With a blush, she decided that he could increase the intensity level but not bare her bottom. It seemed right to keep her panties on for propriety's sake, though she recognized the double standard as her panties might come off for a massage. At the end, when she clicked send, she almost couldn't believe that she did it. Should she call and cancel?

The thought of cancelling drifted through her mind numerous times a day over the next week. Several times she almost picked up the phone to cancel, but a deeper part of her really wanted to keep the appointment. It was out of desperation more than anything else—she wanted to know what it was really like. Alice was ready to stop living in the world of fantasy and see if the reality was all she had hoped it to be. As Mike had told her during the massage, sometimes the reality is quite different than the fantasy.

Alice almost cancelled when she was in the line at

the store to buy a knee-length plaid skirt, she almost cancelled when she was stuck in traffic driving home from work, and she picked up the phone to cancel when she went to the bathroom during her Sunday church service. What right did a married, Christian woman have with paying some stranger to spank her bottom? Even if she had craved it her whole life and didn't think that her husband would understand?

When she was lying in bed the night before the appointment, Alice decided that a big part of her guilt was her inability to tell her husband. Not telling him was pure cowardice, she knew, but she couldn't bring herself to tell him. It wasn't something she could un-say if he reacted badly, and she didn't think that she could take it if he looked at her like there was something wrong with her. He would be kind—he always was. But she just couldn't handle him thinking less of her. What if it changed what he thought about who she was? Alice didn't think she could take his pity, and if he was disappointed in her, it would kill her. But not telling him also felt like a sham.

"Have you told me everything about yourself?" she asked him as they snuggled down for the night.

"Hmm, everything interesting," he replied. "I mean, I may not have told you about my ninth-grade birthday party just because it's boring."

"What if I haven't told you everything?" she asked.

"What? Do you have a Swiss bank account?"

"With millions, of course," she answered easily. Then, after a pause, she tried again. "I think that people are complicated. I'm not sure if I'll ever tell you everything about myself."

"Why not?" he asked. "It's not like I'd love you any

less."

"Maybe I'm not ready," she replied.

He snorted. "If you're not ready, I'm not sure who would be. Aren't you sort of an expert on these things?"

"I am," she answered a bit flummoxed.

"Well, if you have secrets you're working your way up to telling me, it's fine," Barney answered. "Just as long as whatever you do, you tell me is the truth."

"Of course, I would !" she answered mildly surprised.

"Okay then," he replied wrapping one arm around her waist. "Just tell me when you feel ready. But you know, it won't change anything."

"But what if it does?" she asked softly. "What if I told you something that changed how you think of me?"

"Then we go from there," he answered softly. "But everything I've found out about you has made me more excited to be your husband. I don't think anything changes that."

And that right there was why she knew that she married the right man.

CHAPTER THREE

Alice left work early on the day of her spanking and drove to the place with a small bag containing her costume. The costume wasn't sexy or suggestive, because she strove for authenticity. The heavy, wool, plaid skirt had pleats going nearly to her knees. She wore a plain, white shirt and a small tie, as well as thick, white, knee-high socks, and sensible black shoes. For underneath her skirt she had selected a pair of sensible white panties. Alice debated on her hair because she was supposed to be a high school senior, but in the end, she put it into two braids. Braids were easier anyway, and it did add a level of cuteness to the ensemble.

Though they had offered her pick of their costumes (for a fee, or course), she felt more comfortable assembling her own knowing it would fit and meet the specifications she wanted it to have. As she put it on though, she found herself blushing uncontrollably. Was she really dressing up in a costume to go and get her backside spanked by a massage therapist? The very idea.

Leaving the changing room, Alice waiting in a small, very ordinary office for what she assumed as a very extraordinary meeting. Was she really going to have the conversation she assumed she was going to have sitting on beige office chairs? Alice jumped in fright as a knock rapped on the door, and she managed to squeak out a "Come in!"

"Good afternoon, Alice," Mike greeted her. "I thought I might see you back here. Nice skirt."

"Thanks," she answered blushing.

"For first-timers, I like to go over some of our policies to make sure you understand. I know you've read our literature and signed all the consents, but did you have any questions?"

"No, it was all pretty clear," she answered. Her stomach was jumpier than before a performance review at work.

"Okay, then I want to go over safewords again. Think of it like a stoplight, and your stop word is red. If you say red everything stops instantly and doesn't resume unless you say so. You're in control."

She nodded under his firm gaze.

"But you can also say yellow, which can mean that the swats are too hard or that you're in an uncomfortable position. Sometimes people fantasize about being over someone's knee and in reality, it hurts their stomach, or they don't like the feeling of being held during their spanking, and it's better to shift them to bending over the desk or the sofa."

"Sounds good," she said nearly choking.

"When I enter the room, we are in the scene," he explains. "Only your safewords will stop it. All right?"

"Okay," she answered.

"Good," he smiled. "Go ahead and go in the room now, and I'll be in shortly."

Alice nodded, her throat too tight to speak, and made her way to room number twelve, the principal's office. The room had been arranged with some level of detail with a sturdy, antique oak teacher's desk, dark leather sofa, and even details like a school calendar on the wall. She felt for all intents and purposes like a naughty schoolgirl waiting for the principal to return and punish her wrongdoings. Her stomach clenched in anticipation.

There was a sharp knock at the door.

"Come in," Alice managed to squeak out.

"I see you've been sent to me for discipline," Alice heard a stern voice behind her intone. "Miss Brown, I admit I'm surprised to see you here. You've always followed the rules until now."

"Yes, sir," she whispered, not sure of how to answer.

"And yet, I find that you skipped several classes yesterday with no excuse or note from your parent. Can you tell me why that is?"

"No, sir," she answered softly.

"What were you doing instead of attending class?" he asked firmly.

"Just hanging out," she answered wondering what a teen would be doing that wasn't smoking or meeting a boyfriend, and those seemed like the wrong answers to give.

"I see, and not forthcoming to boot," he snapped. "Well, Miss Brown, you leave me little choice. I'm going to administer a spanking to you to encourage you to not engage in this sort of behavior."

"Can't I just have a detention, sir?" she asked with a squeak.

"No. This is a serious infraction," he told her. "Your parents have signed the permission slip, so this is what is going to happen."

"Sir, I . . ."

"You cannot talk your way of this situation, Miss Brown," he told her firmly walking to the sofa and sitting with a squeak of leather. "Put yourself over my lap."

Alice watched as he arranged a pillow on his left, and he motioned Alice to bend over. "Keep your feet on the ground and put your head on the pillow," he instructed firmly.

Gulping with a real fear bubbling in her stomach, she slowly made her way to stand beside his lap. Gently, he helped her bend over in the right position and settled her firmly on his lap wrapping one arm around her waist. She felt trapped, but deliciously so. His lap felt firm under her stomach, and she couldn't shake the feeling that this was make-believe.

"You aren't going to feel my efforts through this skirt," he intoned flipping it easily out of his way. Her bottom was now upturned and bared except for her sensible white panties. She felt her face grow hot.

"You have been very naughty," he told her, and she felt the first slap smack her bottom. The swat wasn't much harder than what he had given her during the massage, and she felt the resultant tingle across her skin. And another slap landed on the other cheek, slightly firmer.

"Please, sir," she asked feeling chastened but playful. "Please no more."

"We have barely begun," he answered with two quick slaps to her backside. She let him continue and then he thoroughly and methodically spanked her entire backside with firm but not harsh spanks. He lifted one leg up and the other down, tipping her at a more precipitous angle.

"You really have been very naughty," he lectured as he adjusted her position. "And if I see you in here again, I might choose to use a ruler on you. You are far too old to be doing these shenanigans."

"Yes, sir," she replied wiggling a bit.

"Hold still," he told her firmly. "I'm now going to spank your sit spots."

She didn't really know what he was talking about, but then she felt a fresh assault on the tender area where her bottom met her upper thighs. She gasped in surprise, and found her legs kicking in response.

"Hold still," he told her firmly. "You deserve this."

"Ow, ow, ow!" She protested with every smack trying to hold herself still but squirming just the same. It didn't hurt enough for her to really be being a baby about it, but it somehow felt good to protest.

"If you can hold still the spanking will be finished at ten more smacks," he told her firmly. "If you wiggle it will be twenty."

"Yes, sir," she replied, a knot of disappointment that it would soon be over.

"One, two . . ." he counted, and of course Alice wiggled and kicked as he smacked her tender upper thighs.

"Very well, Miss Brown," he sighed with disappointment. "Twenty it is."

She squirmed more as he made his way to twenty, and she found her bottom feeling nice and warm. A feeling of need and desire built deep inside her.

"Twenty," he said. "Your punishment is complete, Miss Brown."

"Thank you, sir," she told him sniffing dramatically and pushing herself off his lap. She felt a sense of loss as she stood.

"I expect an apology for your behavior now, or you're going back over her knee for another twenty," he told her sternly. "And they will be even firmer than those swats."

Alice considered. She realized that he was giving her the option to be done. Her bottom was quite warm and slightly stinging. Had she had enough? Part of her said that she did, and not to press her luck. The idea of even firmer smacks made her stomach squirm, but she also knew that she wasn't ready to end the experience.

"I can't apologize if I did nothing wrong," she found herself answering, almost despite herself.

"Another twenty, then," he nodded. "Over my knee, Miss Brown."

She put herself back into position, and as he flipped up her skirt she squirmed and wondered if she had made the best decision. She had a feeling that this was going to hurt a bit more than before.

"You really know better, Miss Brown," he scolded as he adjusted her position. "But if I must redden your bottom to get you to behave, that is what I will do."

She didn't answer but felt his hand slap firmly against her bottom. That elicited a soft yelp from her, and she found herself squirming. The hand that wrapped around her waist constricted to hold her tightly, and his palm began raining down on her bottom firmly. She kicked and squirmed protesting her innocence, but Mike was made of solid concrete for all it affected him. The smacks fell quickly, and she felt the heat build on her stinging backside.

"Now Miss Brown," he said firmly when the spanks stopped. "I'm going to keep you in this position until you apologize. But I must warn you, if you continue in this stubborn resistance, I will be forced to take more drastic measures. Up until now I have not been swatting you very hard at all, but I will increase the intensity and spank your sit spots rosy if you do not apologize."

"Please, sir," she said politely. Alice hesitated and decided to throw caution to the wind. "You cannot make me apologize."

"Very well, Miss Brown," he curtly answered.

She couldn't believe that she chosen more. It felt surreal. He raised one leg and lowered the other again as before, and she gasped in trepidation.

"That's right, Miss Brown," he told her sharply. "This is how misbehavior is dealt with here. I do not know how your parents deal with this sort of blatant disobedience, but this is how it's dealt with here. I will continue your spanking until you apologize, no matter how red your bottom becomes."

And with that, his hand began slapping her sit spots much more firmly. She wiggled and protested, yelped and squirmed, and still the firm hand continued slapping exactly where it intended. The hand curled around the curve of her bottom, wrapping around the tender edge, inflicting heat and sting. She closed her eyes against the sting, but still the hand kept slapping with relentless perseverance. Suddenly everything around felt dimmer somehow, and she even forgot that her nearly naked bottom was being spanked by a virtual stranger. All she could feel was the rhythm, and how it continued. Finally, something inside her broke open and she felt a sob come from deep within herself.

"I'm sorry!" she said, her legs going limp. "I'm sorry!"

The spanking instantly stopped, and she felt his hand gently begin rubbing her back. Tears leaked out her eyes, but she also felt elated and deeply touched. It was like nothing she'd ever felt before.

"Really, all this fuss, and you just needed to apologize," Mike said firmly. "It's all right, Miss Brown. Sometimes people just need to cry a bit."

And with that she did cry a little, still face-down over his lap, her skirt up and her panties all that were protecting her. She was sure her bottom must be a dark shade of scarlet after all those slaps, but she was surprised how fast the sting was fading after the application of the hand was finished. Alice felt a tissue being pressed into her hand, and her breathing began to return to normal as she dabbed her eyes.

"There, there Miss Brown," he said gently. "There, there. You took that punishment well, and I'm sure you won't repeat that infraction. Here, let's lay you down on the couch."

Her skirt found its way back down, and she was soon lying face-down on the couch. He began rubbing her back softly, murmuring comforting things to her. She felt his hands gently massage her shoulders and back, and then in a business-like way slide under her skirts and begin massaging her thighs and buttocks. Though her eyes were closed, she could tell he dimmed the lights and put on soothing music. As his hands rubbed away the last of the sting, she found herself sighing in contentment. She faded away from the naughty schoolgirl and back into the massage therapy client.

Alice wanted to ask Mike why she wanted that, and why it felt so good to be over his knee. But she didn't. She found herself wanting to curl up into her shame place again as well but stopped herself. Just for a moment she wanted to enjoy that she chose to enact the fantasy she had for so long.

Gradually, the massage ended, and she heard Mike say softly, "Take as long as you need, Miss Brown." And she knew, that time lying down with soothing music wasn't all she needed.

Alice needed to come back.

CHAPTER FOUR

And so, her double life began. She wanted to try everything, do everything, and experience everything. She set up bi-weekly therapeutic appointments under the guise of self-care and found the thoughts of her time there filling up the rest of her week.

Even in moments where it was completely inappropriate, like when she was supposed to be concentrating on what her clients were saying, she found herself dreaming about the therapeutic appointments. And there were so many fun scenarios to choose from—why would anybody choose a regular spanking when they could be a princess? Or a cowgirl? Or an English governess?

"I'm tired of the double life," Alice's client told her catching Alice off guard and startling her out of her therapeutic mindset.

"That makes sense," she affirmed trying not to appear ruffled.

"I feel like trying to keep it in is harder than anything else," the client continued. "I mean, I started off thinking that it would be better for people not to know that he was saying those things to me, right? I mean, my sister would be so hurt to know that her husband was doing that, and the only way to have her not find out was to not tell anyone. I know if I told my parents they wouldn't stand up for me. They would probably blame me for what I was wearing or something."

"It sounds like it leaves you in such a bad place, though."

"It does," she admitted. "It's like he knows he can say anything he wants to me, and nobody will do anything about it; I'm powerless."

"He's taking advantage of that."

"He is!" she agreed. "Cassie doesn't know it, but if I told her it would kill her."

"She's an adult," Alice gently reminded her.

"And my baby sister," the client pushed back but then crumpled. "I can't believe she's married to that man."

"Do you think that Cassie knows about him?"

"I don't," her client shook her head. "She's always talking about how amazing he is. I don't know if I'm the only one he does it to or what, but I don't think she knows."

"You seem so trapped."

"I just don't know what to do."

"What do you want to do?"

"I want to yell at him and tell him that he can keep all his horrible comments to himself!" she snarled, a glint in her eye. "I want to tell him that I don't care what he thinks her ass looks like!"

"That sounds really powerful!"

"But I'm not that powerful," she admitted, the glint gone.

The heaviness of that admission hung between them.

"And I want my parents to say that he can't talk to their daughter that way," she admitted looking away. "Part of me wants to be strong and defend myself, and the other part of me wants to know that they have my back, you know? But Rick knows that they don't have my back, he knows I'm a good victim."

That client and Alice had a lot to unpack in that session, but her desperation to not live a double life caught Alice in its intensity. For her, it was to escape her brother-in-law's abuse and harassment; but Alice found echoes in her own story. Would she always be in her own double life? Would she ever be able to tell her husband?

The next day Alice had a therapeutic session, and she found herself with those deep questions that she really didn't want to ponder. She wanted to be a medieval princess being spanked for misbehaving at a formal dinner, not asking questions about her identity and the prospects of a double life.

Alice was able to push her questions away long enough to enjoy the spanking, and when she was lying down afterwards, her bottom stinging nicely from a well-applied wooden hairbrush that she had grown to truly love, the questions came back.

"Why?" she asked in a voice so soft that Mike could pretend that he didn't hear it if he wanted to.

Mike sighed but kept his attention to her muscles ongoing. "Do you remember what I said when we first met?"

She nodded.

"I meant that," he told her. "Some people are just built this way. My first client that wanted this, she was a smart one. Looked up all kinds of research and such—found that science hasn't really found a reason for people to be like they are. It's not due to abuse or trauma or anything like that, it's just kind of how you're built."

"But I feel so guilty," she said.

"Lots of folks do until they accept it," he said matter-of-factly. "I see all kinds in here, I'm sure you can imagine."

"But how do I stop feeling this way?"

"Tell your husband," Mike sighed.

"Do what?"

"Tell your husband," he repeated patiently. "Clearly you haven't. You probably haven't told anybody unless I miss my guess. If he's any sort of a decent guy, he can help you a lot with this guilt. Might even strike a client off my list, if you know what I mean."

"Do you think so?"

"Listen, some people come here because they just want a spanking for stress relief or they don't have a partner," he said finishing the massage and the leaning back. "I don't think you're in that category. If you have a good partner, someone who is willing and understands, this is better done in that kind of partnership. You at least owe him a chance to come through for you on this."

"But what if he doesn't understand, or he thinks it's wrong?"

"Then come back to me!" Mike grinned. "But I think he might surprise you. Look, there's a part to spanking for a lot of people that I can't provide for you."

"What's that?"

"You go home and have a rocking good roll in the hay afterwards, don't you?"

"How do you know that?" she asked, flummoxed.

"I've been doing this a while," he answered. "There's a sexual component for a lot of people, and that's something that I can't help you with. That's your husband's territory."

"But is it wrong?" she asked. "Is it a sin?"

"Look, I'm no priest," Mike said. "I'm a little like a bartender, really, and one that's a lapsed Catholic that currently attends Presbyterian with his wife, so take that into consideration. So, I'll give you her opinion if you promise not to take my words as scripture, okay?"

"Okay."

"Well, it's not like there's anything against it in the Bible, right?"

"Not that I know about."

"Okay, so then, why would it be a sin? Just because you enjoy it?"

"Maybe . . ."

"Is it hurting anybody?"

"Well . . ." Alice smirked as she rubbed her bottom.

"Of course," he chuckled. "So, you're saying it's not forbidden in the Bible, it doesn't hurt anyone really, and why would it be a sin then?"

"I guess I just feel so guilty that it's hard to believe it's not a sin."

"Don't confuse sin with guilt," he said. "There's tons of folks that have guilt and shame that don't have sin to go with it, and tons of folks that have tons of sin with no guilt and shame. One is not always a good indicator of the other. And it's not a sin to be who God created you to be."

As Alice dressed, she thought about what Mike said. Was he right? Did she owe Barney a chance to come through for her? It was nearly impossible to envision Barney being okay with that part of herself as she was barely okay with it. Was Mike right that she was confusing sin with shame? What if he said that she was a big sinner and had to stop? Could she stop? Could she stop writing?

Pictures of when she had tried to stop writing floated before her eyes— it had been such a hard time. Alice became convinced that her stories were sinful and that she had to stop writing them, so she burned them. It had been a damp Saturday in May, the foggy woods surrounded her, and with a little lighter fluid soon the notebooks reduced to nothing but ashes and charred spirals. She had hoped that sacrifice, that burnt offering would appease an ancient god and he would remove the thorn from her side, but that was not to be. The thorn stayed firmly in place, and in fact with no outlet, the stories became increasingly harder to control. Characters and details pulled at the edges of her conscious mind all the time, as if they knew that their survival relied on her memory once that they did not have the permanency of being enshrined in acres of lined paper.

For the next few years she didn't find deliverance or redemption, instead finding it increasingly difficult to get her psyche under control. Alice eventually gave in and began writing again simply to get the stories out of her head, otherwise they threatened to distract her from everything else. It was in guilt and shame that she wrote, and she wrote as little as possible. But still, she didn't want to give that up.

Was Mike right?

Kate stared at her computer screen finding it difficult to continue with the story. Why did she always get so stuck there? Whenever Alice came to the point of telling Barney, she didn't know what to do with her. Should she tell? Would Barney love her anyway? She knew Barney would, because in her worlds, characters always had a happy ending, but for some reason being able to envision what exactly that world would look like was difficult. And that story was different than the story about the Scottish lass wed in secret to the stern, older Laird, or the English Governess who married the older son returning from war, as well. Alice's story made no pretenses. There was no talk of corsets and kilts to get in the way at all. That, time, that story was about her and Jason. Sure, Emerald City Massage was a delicious figment of her own imagination, but she definitely lived a double life that her husband knew nothing about. And she had no idea how to tell him.

CHAPTER FIVE

"Things were good today at work, right?" Jason asked as he cut into the pot roast that had been sensibly cooking in the crock pot all day. "Does that mean you're into, well, having some fun tonight?"

"Yes," Kate answered with a smile trying to put all the confusing questions out of her head. "That would be really nice."

"I was thinking about what you were saying about sexual fantasies," he said, obviously a bit embarrassed as he picked up his glass of iced tea. "I mean, when we were talking the other day?"

"I remember," she answered, her breath getting a

little tight. Was he going to reveal something?

"Well, I just wanted you to know how much I love you wearing something sexy," he told his wife locking eyes with her purposefully. "Do you think I could talk you into some negligee for the evening?"

"I think I can be persuaded," Kate answered with a coy smile. "Why don't you get the dishes put away quickly, and I'll go get the bedroom ready?"

Slipping into a negligee that she knew he liked, Kate thought about the fact that if she truly was Alice her bottom would have been paddled by Mike today and she would be enthusiastic about having sex with her husband that night. How would Alice tell Barney? Would Barney feel that going to get spanked by a massage therapist to be cheating? Kate looked at the nightie she wore in the mirror and frowned at it. It was a sheer black confection, barely skimming her admittedly overly abundant curves and looking ready for action, but it wasn't what she had in mind. Slipping it off, she put on the nightie that had a lacey black top and a sheer plaid skirt on it. The plaid skirt reminded her of the schoolgirl outfit in her story, and somehow that made her feel racier.

"You lit candles," Jason remarked as he entered the room. "Hmm, you look nice in that."

"Well I think the point isn't that I wear it too long," Kate answered with a smile. Jason really was a kind husband, she told herself watching him eagerly shed his clothes in anticipation.

"Come here, then," he told her gruffly heading toward the bed. "Let's see what we can do about that."

His mouth met hers engulfing her tongue. Her body felt weightless as he lifted her onto the bed. His hands roamed gently to her breasts feeling the nipples through the soft fabric of the lacey nightie. "Oh, this feels so soft on you," he said, his mouth breaking off the kiss and kissing softly up her neck.

Kate, molding her body to his as his fingers began to explore lower on her body, suddenly arched as his fingers met their target. He caressed softly, teasingly, expertly knowing the amount of touch she liked. The nightie was gone like a whisper leaving only bare skin touching.

"Right there," she groaned wrapping her arms around his neck. "Oh, baby."

Kate put all thoughts of Alice out of her head as she let herself be swept away in the loving, gentle caresses of her husband as they made love. With the final firm thrusts of him inside of her, she yelled as the wave of pleasure overtook her, and her husband groaned in his own release a few strokes later. Sinking on her, his member still inside her, they held onto each other in exhausted fulfillment.

"Hmm," Jason hummed against her. "You seemed to like that."

"Well, you know, I just put up with it to keep you happy," she laughed softly back at him. It was an old joke, back from when most of the marriage books they had read seemed to make it seem as if the wife didn't enjoy sex as much as the husband, but to their surprise she did. "My wifely duties, you know."

"Good wifey, then," he told her disengaging himself with a gentle kiss to her forehead and placing a hand towel where he had been. Kate curled her back to him, the invitation to spoon which was accepted with gentleness. Kate loved that sweaty, cozy afterglow when her thighs still twitched with her orgasm and her body felt as relaxed as over-cooked spaghetti.

"I thought maybe we could plan a trip to that inn on the island," Jason told her softly. "You know, the one with the big tub. Your talk about sexual fantasies made me wonder if you were thinking about doing that kind of a thing."

Kate knew what he meant— it was a recent development that he had been okay with exploring oral sex, and it made him a lot more comfortable to do it either in or directly after they had had a bath together. That inn he was talking about had a lovely large tub, and a king-sized four poster bed with mirrored tiles on the ceiling. It certainly made her feel naughty to have sex there.

"That sounds really nice," she answered. "But it's not my birthday or anything special. What are we celebrating?"

"Didn't that engagement class say we should have nights away sometimes?"

"I thought that was for when we have kids."

"Well, maybe we should practice," he laughed. "I got a spot bonus from one of my colleagues and it should just about cover it, and I think this is how I'd like to spend it. Doesn't it sound like fun?"

"It does," Kate answered snuggling in. "It sounds like a lot of fun. Let's do it."

"Was there anything else you wanted to try?" he asked caressing her arm softly. "I mean, how you keep bringing it up makes me wonder."

"Wonder what?" Kate asked suddenly very alert.

"Wonder if you're trying to tell me something that I'm not getting because I'm kind of an oblivious guy."

"What if there was something?" she asked, her voice

soft.

"Well, I would hope you could tell me eventually," he said.

"What if I worried that it would change how you think of me?"

"I can't image how it would," he answered seriously. "I mean, is it something like you were abused as a kid or something? Or something you've done that you're worried about?"

"No, you know everything about that."

"Well, I can't imagine anything changing how I feel," he said in seriousness. "I love you; I don't think that changes. But I don't want you to feel pressure, anything you tell me has to be the right time to tell me."

"Did anyone ever tell you that you were the best husband ever?" Kate told him snuggling into him softly.

"All my wives tell me that," he smiled back.

"Well, you're in my top five, that's for sure," she laughed.

"Great," he said. "I'm going to get up and brush my teeth." Jason reached over and landed a playful swat on Kate's backside, and the effect was electric. Even though there was barely a sting, it was as if she felt the effects all over her body. What she wouldn't give for him to do that more! And therein also was the rub— if he knew how much she craved that, how much she wanted that, would he stop doing it if she felt it was bad? Would she lose the occasional playful swat she got from him when she teased him?

Changing into her more sensible cotton nightgown and joining him to brush her own teeth, Kate began to think about what the night away at the inn could look like if she had a husband who would spank her. She could come out of the tub, her skin pink from the warmth, and towel off just to bend over the edge of that massive four poster bed . . .

"Are you daydreaming?" Jason asked laughing at her. "Earth to Kate! Hello?"

"I'm here!" she answered, chagrined. "Sorry, I was just thinking about going to the inn this weekend. I hope we get the room with the four-poster bed with the little mirrors on the ceiling."

"I will call tomorrow and try and get it," he promised. "I'm going to look forward to it all week."

"Me too," she blushed.

CHAPTER SIX

Alice knew she had to tell Barney. Mike was right.
But how to do it? Could it just be a sexy utterance while they
were on their fun night away? Should it be some serious
discussion when they were somewhere where he could get
away and have some time to himself if he needed it? What
should she do? Would she regret it?

That night at dinner, she watched him eat his pizza
with relish. He always loved that little place around the
corner. A talk like that should happen on pizza night.

"So, I was thinking about how to tell you something,
and I think I should just come out and say it," Alice said
picking at a pepperoni on her own slice.

"Sure," he answered wiping tomato sauce off his
lower lip. "What's up?"

"Well, you know how we were talking before . . ."

"Oh, is this the thing you were worried about telling
me?" he said suddenly at full attention.

"Yes," she agreed. "Well, you see, ever since I was

a young girl, I've always had a very specific fantasy. I don't know why I have this fantasy, and it really embarrasses me. I'm not even sure there's a sexual component to it or not, but I think there might be; I know there is for other folks."

"Okay, lay it on me," Barney said eating the last bite of his pizza.

"Well, I've always wanted to be spanked," Alice told him, breathless at her own bravery. It was out of her mouth; the rest was up to him. She felt her legs tingle; she was ready to run.

"What, like a little kid?" he asked confused.

"Yes," she answered feeling as if there were a belt tightening, strangling her throat.

"Well, that's messed up," he said looking at his wife in shock.

"I had hoped . . ." Alice started.

"I had thought you wanted to talk about oral sex again or something," he said. "I mean, that's not what I expected you to say. Aren't you a therapist? Shouldn't you be more fixed than this?"

"What?" Alice replied, tears springing to her eyes.

"This is like BDSM, isn't it?" he accused. "This is sin, it's broken and wrong. I can't believe that you think this is an okay fantasy, and you were asking me as if I would participate with you."

"Barney . . ."

"We need to call the pastor, pronto," he said. "There are some serious problems here. We need to have a serious talk with him. Are you telling me that when I swatted your bottom in fun *you got off on that*? Well, clearly, we're not doing that anymore."

"But Jason . . ."

Kate stopped the story in shock, tears springing to her own eyes and when she realized that she had typed "Jason" instead of "Barney" into the story. That was her worst nightmare, and everything Barney said to Alice in that scenario were things that she had said to herself, maybe a hundred times. But even as her fingers clicked along on the keyboard, she knew that the gentle lover and kind Barney in that story wasn't the type of man to do that to his wife when she revealed something so personal and difficult for her. She knew Barney was probably more like Mike, and certainly kinder. She quickly deleted the scene, giving Alice another chance.

"Well, I've always wanted to be spanked," Alice told him, breathless at her own bravery. It was out of her mouth; the rest was up to him. She felt her legs tingle; she was ready to run.

"Thank you for telling me," Barney told her putting his hand on hers. "I can see why that was so hard to tell me."

"Then you understand?" she asked, hopeful tears springing to her eyes. Was it possible he understood her?

"Of course," he said. "We are all broken on the inside, and it must be so hard to share that brokenness with me. And it comes from such a young part of you too. Oh, my dear, I'm so sorry."

"Sorry?" Alice echoed with a hollow voice.

"Have you figured out what childhood abuse caused it?" he pressed gently.

"No, not actually," she demurred.

"Well, then there's work to be done," he said patting

her hand reassuringly.

"But I was thinking differently about it," Alice replied, suddenly uncomfortable. "I mean, I was thinking about it, and what if it is just something about me that's different? What if it's like me liking spicy food or something? What if it's not brokenness and shame?"

"But my dear, of course it's shameful," he answered earnestly. "Of course, it's brokenness. What else could it be?"

"What if it's just something, I don't know, something fun to do?" she asked. "Like, what if we could . . ."

"You don't think we could actually, well, engage in that sort of thing, do you?" he asked with a slight mocking in his voice. "That I would actually spank you? And you would, I don't know, get off on it? Clearly that's sick and twisted. You need help."

"Maybe I do," Alice replied miserably.

"I mean really, you're a feminist, aren't you?"

"Yes," she answered, feeling as far from a woman with agency as she had ever felt.

"My brave girl," he soothed stroking her hair lovingly. "We need to get you back into therapy right away."

Kate broke off again. That was a kinder and gentler Barney, but she still hated him. He was patronizing and smug, and not the gentle lover that he had been during the first part of the story. That wasn't him, and she knew that that wasn't her husband either. Barney was clearly her husband on paper, and she wasn't getting him right, yet. She had to try again.

"Well, I've always wanted to be spanked," Alice told him, breathless at her own bravery. It was out of her mouth; the rest was up to him. She felt her legs tingle; she was ready to run.

"Okay," Barney replied rubbing his hands with the paper napkin. "Would you like to try it tonight?"

"What, just like that?" Alice asked incredulously.

"Why not?" he asked. "I mean, if it's something you've always wanted to try, why not give it a try and see what it does for you? I admit I'm curious now myself."

"But you can't just be this okay with it!" she nearly yelled. "You're not even okay with oral sex, and you're okay with this?"

"The oral sex thing is just because, well, I'm worried about the hygiene of it," he answered affably. "This seems different. Goodness gracious, Alice, you're acting as if you want me to reject you. Don't you want to try it out?"

She started at him, dumbfounded at the expression of his love for her and feeling absolutely and profoundly accepted. Could it really be this thing that she had dreaded for so long could be that easy in the face of a loving husband?

"Let's try it out," she agreed with him. "Bedroom?"

"So, my old man only spanked me a few times," Barney said as they went to the bedroom together, pizza dishes forgotten. "I bent over his lap and he smacked my backside. Do you think like that?"

"Maybe I should bend over the bed," Alice said. "That might be easier."

"Okay," he agreed. "So, we're naked, right?"

"Sounds good," she agreed with a smirk. "Things

are always more fun naked."

As Alice quickly divested herself of her clothes, it seemed unreal that she would actually be doing this. Was her actual husband going to actually spank her? In no time she was naked, bending over the bed, and wondering what a spanking from her inexperienced husband was going to feel like . . .

"Whatcha doing?" Jason asked coming up from behind Kate and attempting to hug her while she sat at her desk.

"Aack!" she yelled in surprise clamping down her laptop in desperate haste.

"What were you working on?" he asked, surprised at her reaction.

"Nothing!" Kate answered, her face clearly saying the opposite.

"Look, Kate," Jason said sitting in the chair beside her. "It's okay if there's something you don't want me to see. We can have the porn talk."

"It wasn't porn!" she insisted, indignant.

"Then what was it that you didn't want me to see?" he asked confused. "You don't act like that when it's just work stuff."

"Just writing a story," she answered. "You startled me."

"A story?" he asked leveling his eyes at his wife. "Can I read it?"

That was a gambit, and Kate knew it. He never read her stories; he really had no interest in them. He only read books by Dick Francis and Terry Pratchett, and so he let her hum along writing stories he assumed were just romantic fluff.

"Why would you want to?" Kate asked. "You never have before."

"Your reaction," he shrugged. "It just made me wonder a bit. Don't worry, I'm not going to hack your computer or anything. I just wanted to see if you would be okay with it. It's fine that you're not."

"I didn't say that I wasn't!" she protested.

"You didn't have to," he replied. "It's kind of obvious. Is this connected with that thing you wouldn't tell me about the other day?"

"Yes," she answered looking away with chagrin.

"And so, the mystery deepens," he said with a wry smile.

"I should just tell you," she told him looking back at the man that sat beside her.

"Only if you're ready," he told her. "I'm not trying to push you."

"I don't know when I'll be ready," Kate told him honestly.

"It's okay," he said. "But I'll be here when you're ready."

CHAPTER SEVEN

"Excited about going to the inn this weekend?" Jason asked as they crawled into bed together. Teeth had, of course, brushed their teeth, started the dishwasher, and watched the obligatory Netflix show.

"Yep," Kate answered. "You did say we got the room we wanted, right?"

"Yes," he answered. "And we got a free bottle of wine, too, because they're running some promotion about repeat customers or something."

"That's nice."

"Well, it's probably a six-dollar bottle, but it's a nice gesture."

"What do you want to do this weekend?" she asked. "Make use the tub?"

"Among other things," he answered wiggling his eyebrow. "What sort of naughtiness can we get up to there?"

"All sorts of fun things," Kate agreed.

"Want a little preview?" Jason asked, gently caressing her back as she lay on the bed. "We could, you know, practice a bit?"

"Of course," she answered smiling at his invitation.

He began kissing her coaxing her out of her cotton nightgown and stroking her back softly. Pushing Kate's long, brown curls out of the way, he kissed her soft skin. Kate felt her husband's caresses and thought about what he had said earlier in the day. She wondered if she really could tell him about the Spanking Sin. Would he be like the third imagining of Alice's encounter with Barney? Or like one of the others? But here, in their room together, it felt really safe—safe enough to be honest.

"So, you know that thing that I wanted to tell you?" Kate said hardly able to believe the words were coming from her mouth.

"Yes," he answered nuzzling her neck.

"Well, it actually has to do with fantasy," she told him. "Do you want to hear it?"

"Sure," he said remaining casual. She could tell he was trying hard not to spook her, and that made it feel easier.

"Well, since I was a young girl, I've always had a very specific fantasy," she admitted. "I'm not sure if it's a sexual fantasy or not, but I think it might be. So, you see, I've always wanted to be spanked."

"Spanked?" he asked. "That's the big secret?"

Kate nodded, not able to speak from the adrenaline sparking in her veins. She felt ready to jump out of her skin, to run and never stop, or to at least get out of the bedroom.

"Okay," he nodded. "We can try that."

"Really?" she squeaked, unbelieving.

"Sure," he answered. "I mean, if you want to and everything. Roll over? Oh wait, maybe bend over the bed?"

In complete shock at the outplaying of the conversation, Kate stepped out of bed and bent over the edge. Feeling like she had to pinch herself to prove to herself that she wasn't in one of her stories, she couldn't believe that was happening. How many times had she fantasized about that? How many times had she longed for just that outcome? Would she wake up and find that it was all a dream?

Jason lifted her cotton nightgown and gently pulled down her panties, and Kate shivered in anticipation. How many of her imaginings involved her husband lifting the hem of her skirt? It just had such a delicious feeling to it. He then stroked her bared backside fondly chuckling to himself a little. "How hard should I do it?" he asked, his voice light and teasing.

"I don't know," she answered honestly. "But, you know, don't be afraid for it to be more than a pat."

"How about I give you a swat and you tell me if it's too hard?" he asked.

Kate nodded in agreement finding herself beyond being able to speak well. He slapped her bottom lightly, hardly a slap at all.

"I think harder than that," Kate laughed, her nervousness coming out. "Please?"

"Okay," he answered, and then gave a harder slap. Kate wiggled a bit at this one feeling her body respond a bit more to that one and feeling her skin tingle. "More like that," she told him. "And harder still."

Jason gave her a few more swats, mostly on the upper part of her bottom. "Harder," she told him. "Harder and lower on my bottom."

"If you're sure," he told her aiming a few swats lower on her bottom and with a stronger hand.

Kate closed her eyes and felt the sensation of the spanking with her whole body. Never before had something felt so right before. She began to cry out as the swats landed, and it was becoming very obvious that indeed she was having a physical response to the strikes— a very sexual response. Her hips wiggled back and forth, and she found herself lifting up onto her tiptoes in response to the smacks. It did hurt, but the stinging invoked something deeper— both in her body and in her psyche. It felt amazing.

"Your bottom is getting red," he told her pausing the spanking to caress her bottom softly.

Kate felt him caress her bottom, the desire for him to be inside of her overcoming her, and for that to be as quickly and firmly as possible. She had never felt the urge so strongly; she needed him right then.

"Touch me," she begged spreading her legs wider to accommodate him, her voice husky with need. "Please."

Jason recognized the change in tone, and his hand went deftly to her sensitive parts, where abundant lubrication met his fingertips with a clear welcome. "Please!" Kate asked again, that time was a clear invitation. Always before, foreplay was long and teasing, but this time Kate was demanding. Jason took her up on the invitation, and soon entered her fully from behind, with her still bent over the bed. Kate yelled, not able to stifle her orgasm, and with her hips, she encouraged him to enter deeper.

"Harder," she urged losing herself in the sensations. "Harder."

He obeyed her directions, and soon found himself

thrusting harder and faster to her insistence, until he cried out a few moments later in his own release. He stood there, spent, as he watched his wife, still bent over and panting at her exertions. They had never had a joining like that one—it felt wild and a little reckless.

As Kate lay there trying to catch her breath, she couldn't believe her body's response to the spanking her husband gave her. Clearly it was something she craved, but the intensity of her reaction scared her a little. She had orgasmed, but it was different than any orgasm she ever experienced. It was deeper, wilder, more immediate and intense, and in what felt like a different part of her genitalia. And, much to her embarrassment, her body provided so much lubrication, it dripped down her leg—something that had never occurred before. And what happened to all the gentle foreplay she was used to? That entire encounter had probably taken seven minutes.

"How was that for you?" Jason asked softly, gently disengaging himself, grabbing her a hand towel from the drawer beside the bed and helping her into their usual spooning position.

"Well, that was different," she admitted, barely feeling as if her brain was functional. "I mean, completely wonderful and amazing, but not at all what I was expecting."

"Did I hurt you?" he asked with some concern. "Your bottom did get a little pink."

"A bit," she smiled wiggling against him. "But I would like it to hurt a bit more."

"We have a lot to talk about," Jason said snuggling beside her and enjoying the warmth.

"We do," she agreed. "This changes so much. But for right now, can I just enjoy what this means to me? You have no idea how much this means to me."

"Of course." She reveled in the feel his breath against her neck.

"Thanks for being so great about it," she told him. "You really are the best husband ever."

"Thanks for telling me," he told her. "I know that was hard to do."

"And now we have a whole new sex world to explore together."

It took Kate a long time to fall asleep that night—she lay there listening to her husband snore for a long time as she formulated words and ideas to try and give thought to what just happened to her. Not only did she tell her husband her deepest, darkest secret— one she had vowed to take to the grave without telling any other soul— but he accepted her! And not only that, he participated in her fantasy— he actually spanked her! He loved her and wanted her to be happy, no matter who she was or how she was.

And then there was the spanking itself; she wasn't sure how to unpack that either. Kate lay there, feeling the after-effects of the encounter, and wondering about the type of orgasm and how the encounter worked. The slight tingle on her backside was the only residue of the spanking, and she found herself a little sad that it faded so quickly. She felt much as she had on her wedding night when everything felt exciting and new, and she didn't understand what her body was doing. But she knew two things for sure, and more so than she had ever known anything before: spanking was definitely sexual for her, and there was no giving it up.

CHAPTER EIGHT

"Okay, so I get that you don't understand why you like this," Jason told her reasonably tapping on the steering wheel a little bit as he drove. "But it's pretty clear that you do. Doesn't your psych stuff cover it?"

"What I've found is that some people have it," Kate explained. *Psychology Today* said that there was a study that found that people who are kinky are actually more psychologically well adjusted."

"Okay, so then why was it so hard to tell me?" he asked reasonably.

Kate looked out the window at the salt flats whizzing by and found it hard to explain. "You see, I found out when I was very young that I was different, and I had to keep it secret," she explained. "I never intended to tell you at all."

"Were you worried I'd condemn you?"

"Yeah," she said. "I was worried you'd think I was sinful and sick and wrong. And you know how you give me a pat on the backside every once in a while? I was so afraid those would go away. I just, well, I love you so much that I just couldn't stand you thinking less of me."

"First off, let me say that I don't think this is sinful and sick and wrong," he told her firmly. "I think this is like you said— something that's just a bit spicy about you. I think this could definitely open up some new fun with regard to us having sex. I get that there's some deep shame that hopefully we can work through, but shame doesn't always equal sin, right?"

"Right," she nodded, a little dumbfounded by her normally theologically-adverse husband spouting exactly what she needed to hear.

"God wants us to live in freedom, not mired down in shame," he told her with confidence. "You're the one that's always telling me that."

"Yeah, but it's hard for me to believe that this isn't a sin," I told him. "For so many years I thought I was so broken."

"And if you did have some sin that was a problem, I would hope that we could talk about it, because my job isn't to condemn you either," he told her earnestly. "Remember, we are supposed to be Jesus to each other, and a big part of that is to reassure each other of grace, not to condemn each other."

"You're right," she agreed. "I'm sorry I didn't trust you more."

"It's not a problem," he grinned at her. "You just

needed to get ready, that's all. I just wanted you to know that in case there are any more secrets lurking about."

"No, this is the big one," she reassured him.

"Okay, I have a few questions, then," he said.

"Shoot," she told him. "We have at least an hour until we get to the inn, probably more with this traffic."

"How young did you know?" he asked, curious.

"These are some of my earliest memories," she admitted. "Honestly, it was kindergarten and first grade. When I found stories with spanking in them, I would read them over and over. Eventually, I started writing them."

"But you didn't want to get spanked as a child, though?" he asked. "I remember you telling me that story about you going to great lengths to avoid your mom spanking you."

"I know it sounds weird, but I was only spanked a few times as a kid," she told him. "And it was really awful. I didn't understand why something I dreamed about could be so awful in actuality, but it was really terrible. You know, my sister Jackie would actually ask for a spanking instead of being grounded because it would be over faster— I could never understand her!"

"Well, if it's a part of your sexuality that would make sense," Jason nodded. "I mean, I didn't like getting spanked as a child, but it didn't bother me that much."

"Do you crave a spanking at all?" Kate asked.

"Not at all," Jason admitted. "But don't worry, what turns me on is you getting turned on, so I'm in this game. Tell me about what your fantasies about spanking look like."

"Well, it's usually around a person actually getting in trouble and getting punished," Kate told him. "I mean, now that I told you, I felt some freedom to do a bit more research, and I found some things online. One of my fantasies some people actually do— they call it Domestic Discipline. It sounds so embarrassing to admit, but it seems so hot."

"So, the husband tells the wife she did something wrong and actually punishes her?" Jason asks. "Like, for real?"

"Yep," Kate told him.

"Like, in what kind of a scenario?" he pressed.

Kate tried to remember a scenario that actually sounded legitimate, but suddenly all the situations seemed kind of phony. "Umm, I think maybe for texting and driving? Or she was lazy and didn't do the laundry?"

"Okay, let's actually think about that," Jason said. "I don't think that either of us could actually do the reality of that kind of a situation. Are you telling me that it wouldn't offend your feminist self to have me punish you for something?"

Kate burst out laughing realizing that he was completely correct. There was no way that she was going to let him do that, fantasy or no. "That would be terrible!" she laughed. "Oh my goodness, I would kill you! But I'm telling you, it would be so hot for you to tell me I was naughty and getting a spanking."

"How about we act it out?" Jason reasonably suggested. "I have no problem telling you you're naughty, because you are. And we can make something up, you can even write up a scenario if you want."

"Costumes?" Kate asked, breathless with the possibilities.

"Of course," Jason nodded. "As long as it's nothing too much for me. Halloween rules."

"No tights or makeup," Kate repeated with a laugh reciting their agreed-upon rules for Halloween costumes.

"Okay, so what we did the other night, how far was that off the fantasy you have in your head?" Jason asked.

"Well, it was really good," Kate smiled in remembrance feeling the blood rush to her cheeks in a blush. "I mean, I didn't expect my body to respond like that. Wow."

"Yeah, that was pretty intense," he agreed. "But let's be brutally honest, so we can do even better next time."

"Spanking feels best on my lower cheeks," Kate told him. "And I was crazy turned on. Can you spank me harder?"

"To tell you the truth my hand was stinging a lot," he told her. "I'm not sure I can do it a lot harder."

"Apparently my bottom is tougher than your hand," Kate smirked. "We'll have to get a paddle or something. One of the sites I was on recommended a leather paddle as being one of the best things."

"Where do we get one of those?"

"Well, we could order online, but in time for tonight," she told him. "Is there a sexy shop on the way?"

"There might be," he grinned. "Why don't you have a look on your phone?"

"Only ten minutes away," Kate grinned after a moment. "Can you believe our luck?"

"That will be an adventure in itself," Jason replied with chagrin. "It's not like either of us has ever been in a store like that before. What do you think it's like?"

"I'm sure there will be all sorts of embarrassing things in there," she replied wondering. "I mean, there has to be if they have paddles. Are you sure you want to do this?"

"We can do it," he answered. "I mean, this isn't even our town, right? Nobody to recognize us. We'll just act like we do this every day."

"If you say so," Kate answered, unsure.

"Or we just die of embarrassment and sneak out," he laughed.

"So, there's a few other things I learned from all the websites," Kate continued. "I thought it might be good to talk about them."

"Shoot."

"Okay, they all seem to recommend a safeword."

"What's that?"

"Well, it's a word that either person can say that stops everything," Kate explained. "Like, if we're playing the game and you're spanking me and part of what we're doing is me protesting. Like, that's part of the fun. Well, you might not realize it if I'm serious about wanting to stop it, so we agree on a word that I say that you know I'm serious."

"Like, you say something like 'watermelon' and everything stops?"

"Yeah, pretty much."

"I find it hard to believe that I wouldn't know if you were serious," Jason told her. "I mean, wouldn't I?"

"I think so," Kate agreed. "But everybody says you're supposed to do this, so it seems like we should."

"Watermelon sounds good?"

"Watermelon it is," Kate agreed.

"What else, then?"

"Well," Kate said, hesitating. "The other thing wasn't on a web site. I was just thinking after we did that last time. Like, my orgasm was so different. It was like from a different part of my body, and it felt so good."

"How was it different?"

"It's hard to explain," Kate laughed. "I mean, you only have one part for this, right? This felt further back on my body, and deeper. It wasn't my clitoris really; it was somewhere different. Maybe my G spot? I wasn't sure I really had one. All I know is that it was very different."

"Do you think you could have the other type of orgasm as well afterwards?" Jason asked.

"I think I could," Kate answered. "I think I'd like to try."

"Okay, tell you what," Jason told her. "We're going to stop and buy the paddle in a few minutes, that gives you a few minutes to think. You construct exactly how you'd like this scenario tonight to go in your head and tell me about it after the shop. Then we'll see what we can do to make that happen. How does that sound?"

"That sounds amazing," she replied already drifting off in imagining.

"But you can't imagine so much you're not looking at the GPS," he told her, laughing. "Which exit am I taking?"

"Three miles," she answered. "And Jason?"

"Yes?"

"I brought my Halloween costume in my bag."

"The one where you were the medieval princess?"

"Yes."

"Of course, you did."

The sex shop did indeed have many things in it that neither ever saw before or had only heard about. Trying to look brave and completely cool, Kate walked by the entire wall of vibrating dildos and past the rack of lacey negligees in search of the paddles. She saw bondage gear displayed on the wall in the back and assumed that paddles had to be somewhat near those.

"Are those . . .?" Jason choked out as they passed an end cap.

"Better not to look," Kate hissed back. In some ways the department store cheeriness of the place made it seem even weirder— did they really have an endcap of anal beads? What were anal beads?

Soon they came to a rack of different implements, and Kate tried to look at them scientifically. The rack's structure looked like what she had just bought yoga pants from at Target the past week. Was she actually looking at a teal flogger right then? "Who knew there would be so many types of paddles?" Jason asked.

"I don't want one with a word on it," Kate told him. "That looks silly, and it might give me a blister. What I read said that wooden ones hurt too much and not in a good way; leather ones are a lot better. And not a flogger, that looks like it would hurt too much."

"How about this one?" Jason asked picking up a black leather paddle with the striking surface about the size of an outstretched hand, oval in shape, and plain except for four metal rivets holding it together.

"That looks good," Kate nodded taking it from him. "It feels firm, but the leather is soft. Do you think this would work?"

"Yes, I do," Jason told her, his eyes glinting. "I'll bet that stings a bit."

"Is it expensive?"

"Who cares?" Jason laughed. "Let's get it and get out of here!"

They made their way to the front of the store, where a twenty-something with light lavender hair waited to check people out. It struck Kate as completely shocking that she looked bored. How could a checker be bored in a store like that? "Did you find everything you needed?" she asked in a rote voice.

"We did," Kate answered feeling breathless. "Thanks."

"I'm putting in a notice for an upcoming *Fifty Shades of Grey* women's info night we're having," she said with a little bit of a wink. "It's just a night where we're having an educator come in and women can come and ask questions. It's free."

"Thanks," Kate told her, genuinely touched but also positive she would never come.

The clerk put the purchase in a brown paper bag, they paid without really seeing to total at the register, and it felt as if they ran to the car. Once they were in, neither spoke until the car was safely back in traffic once again.

"I can't believe we did that!!!" Kate exploded laughing and incredulous at the same time.

"I've never been so embarrassed in my life!" Jason agreed. "Do you think they knew we were so shocked?"

"Probably," Kate laughed. "I mean, really, we were like deer in the headlights. I can't believe how embarrassing that was!"

"You mean you aren't going back for the info night?" he teased.

"Not for a million dollars," Kate gasped trying to regain normal breathing. "Thank goodness for online shopping; we are never doing that again!"

"Although, it does sort of start our night away with a little bit of a daring spin," Jason said. "I'm already feeling like we're out of our comfort zone, and we aren't even there yet."

"Let me see the paddle," Kate said reaching around to grab it from where Jason threw it in the back seat of their sensible Toyota Prius.

"It looks well made," Jason told her glancing at it.

"Should be for thirty-eight dollars," Kate replied looking at the receipt. "It is nice and thick; it looks like good leather. Stiff, too."

"How does it feel to have one?"

"Good," Kate answered rubbing the surface of the paddle softly. It did feel good, though a little odd. It was going to spank her later— and maybe for years to come. The thought gave her shivers down her spine.

"And with that, Miss Kate," Jason told her seeing her shivers. "Tell me exactly what you'd like me to do to you tonight."

CHAPTER NINE

Kate rose from the bath, her skin warm and rosy from the scented water. Pulling the soft towel around her, she thought of her husband and smiled. He went to get the wine and secure two glasses. She had a few minutes to get herself ready. Laying on the carved, four-poster bed was her soft, cotton chemise and her velvet gown, which she slipped into quickly. Pulling her long, curly hair up and out of the way, she wondered how well he would be able to do what she had asked. Would it be like she had dreamed about for so many years? She perched on the side of the bed, the new paddle sitting beside her in anticipation.

"I'm back," he announced coming into the room. "I see that you have finished your bath, Milady."

"I have, Milord," she answered. "May I have some of the wine you bring?"

"You may after we have a discussion of some of your recent disobedience," he told her sternly. "I think you know what I'm talking about."

"That wasn't my fault!" she protested. "How was I to know that that would happen?"

"It was your fault, and I am going to punish you for it," he told her. "I am your husband, and it is my responsibility. Now, you need to bend over my lap and lift your skirt, lass."

"It's not fair!"

"You knew this would be the consequence when you did it," he told her. "No use putting it off. I'm going to sit on the bed now, and I expect you to be obedient in this at least."

Jason sat on the bed then, his back against the headboard, and laid the paddle beside him. "No use putting it off," he told her sternly. "Get over here."

"Yes, Milord," Kate answered feeling a little silly but her stomach began to flip in anticipation. She climbed onto the giant bed and lay herself across his lap. His legs felt firm and muscular beneath her stomach, and she grabbed a pillow to put under her head. "You don't have to do it too hard, I wasn't that naughty."

"Your bottom is going to be bright pink with all your naughtiness," he told her. "First with my hand and then the paddle. But first let's get this skirt of yours up."

He pulled up her skirt and then her chemise, something that made Kate gasp with anticipation. She wiggled as the cold air caressed her bare bottom.

"Such naughtiness," he told her, and then began a gentle slapping on her bottom. Kate knew more was coming and enjoyed the gentle stinging and the building rhythm of his smacking. Her bottom was feeling just a little warm, and then he paused.

"And now it's time for the paddle," he told her

causing her stomach to flip in anticipation. "I'll start softer and get harder, tell me if it's too much."

Kate wiggled a bit, and the paddle rubbed a bit on her warmed backside. The leather felt cool and smooth, and then it left, to return with a soft slap and a sting. Kate kicked her legs a little, the impact of the paddle sent electricity through her, and elicited a gasp. The paddle came again and again, building up intensity and a rhythm as it went. Kate found herself kicking a bit in response and crying out. Jason put the paddle aside for a moment caressing her backside.

"There's lots of spankings to go, Milady," he told her, softly rubbing her backside. "But maybe a little break? Spread your legs."

Kate obeyed eagerly, and his fingers found her very eager to welcome them in. She was so wet and ready for him, and she cried out as his fingers penetrated her, and then teased her by caressing and not penetrating.

"Please!" she demanded, bucking toward his hand.

"Not yet," he told her patting her bottom. "There's more spankings before I give you that. Remember? You wanted to be teased a bit, Milady."

"I'm beginning to regret that request," she grumbled, and then cried out as the paddle meted out a new round of smacks. Her legs kicked, her hips bucked, and her bottom heated in a way she didn't know possible.

"Please!" she cried out again. "Please! I want you!"

"You want this?" he asked putting the paddle down again and caressing her, her legs spreading wide and eager for him. He caressed and teased, not giving her exactly what she wanted.

"Yes!" she demanded. "Please!"

"Then get up on the side of the bed," he told her.

"I'm going to give you six more licks, hard. Then I will take you from behind, hard and fast. How does that sound?"

"Yes, please!" she said, eagerly jumping from his lap and bending over the side of the bed, pulling up her skirts in anticipation. She wanted him so badly she could hardly stand it.

The first hard smack connected with a dizzying force, and Kate yelped in response, kicking her legs.

"Is that okay?" he asked, concerned.

"I loved it!" she replied. "But no harder than that."

"Okay, five more!" he told her. "Here you go!"

He gave her those last five smacks hard and fast, just as he said he would, and Kate yelped at the sting. And then his fingers caressed, and before she could wonder how he got his clothes off he was there, filling her fully with himself. The feeling of having him pressed against her stinging backside made her groan with pleasure. He thrust hard and fast, and she felt her body crescendo into a crashing orgasm, with her screaming into a pillow to try and stifle the noise.

Then, as the waves of the crescendo passed, she felt him begin to caress her hips and back, and she knew that he wasn't done. They were going to see if more was possible.

"Let's try," she said with a wicked smile, and stood.

Slipping out of her costume, she faced him and began to kiss, pulling him into bed on top of her. He shed his remaining shirt and jumped after her, the softness of the bed enveloping them, and they clung to each other. He bent to kiss her breasts, and she opened her legs in encouragement. He found her pleasure center and began to caress, entering her slowly and carefully. Kate wrapped her legs around him encouraging him deeper. Finding his rhythm, they were soon in the familiar dance of pleasure between them, and Kate's muffled cries soon echoed around the room as Jason's shuddering groans followed moments later. They lay together afterwards, spent, with Kate just listening to Jason's heartbeat. How did it come to be that she could so thoroughly enjoy something that had brought her so much shame before? Did God want her to have freedom, just as Jason had said? Lying on that soft bed, in the arms of her husband, with her bottom still stinging and her medieval dress strewn on the floor, she could almost believe it.

ABOUT THE AUTHOR

The author is married to an incredible husband, lives in the Pacific Northwest of the United States, has more children than is actually respectable, and identifies more with her main character than she'd like to admit. As a former pastor and current psychotherapist, she is concerned about issues of shame and wrote this book in an effort to work through some of her own issues and maybe be of help to others. Besides, who can resist the challenge of writing hot BDSM sex scenes that are (at least in her opinion) compatible with her Christian and Feminist values?